I wrote this book for my son, Stanley.
Love you pal.

SUPERDAD'S DAY OFF

PHIL EARLE

With illustrations by Steve May

Barrington Stoke

First published in 2017 in Great Britain by
Barrington Stoke Ltd
18 Walker Street, Edinburgh, EH3 7LP

www.barringtonstoke.co.uk

Text © 2017 Phil Earle
Illustrations © 2017 Steve May

Reprinted 2018

A CIP catalogue record for this book is available
from the British Library upon request

ISBN: 978-1-78112-684-4

Printed in China by Leo

This book is super readable for young readers beginning their
independent reading journey.

CONTENTS

CHAPTER 1
WHAT IS NORMAL?

Stanley was a normal boy.

He was a normal height, a normal weight, and his head was full of normal dreams. The same things you and I dream of.

Stanley lived in a normal house with an older sister who was annoying, but normal. Even his dog Bonzo was normal. Bonzo liked bones and walks and cocking his leg in places that made Stanley's mum very cross.

There was nothing about Stanley's life that would make you raise an eyebrow. There was nothing that would make you look twice.

Except for ... Stanley's dad.

His dad, you see, was not normal or ordinary. Far from it.

Stanley's dad was extra-ordinary.

Stanley's dad was a SUPERHERO.

Stanley's dad was Dynamo Dan, the greatest crime-fighter our world has ever seen. Or any other world, for that matter. Day after day, week after week, year after year, Dynamo Dan would save the day.

"Help! Help! A comet is going to crash-land on top of New York City!"

Not today – with Dynamo Dan on hand!

"Oh crikey, oh blimey. Bad guys have kidnapped the Queen!"

Not to worry – here comes Dynamo Dan!

"Oh pooh-sticks. Robbers have stolen a billion pounds from the world's biggest bank!"

They won't get away – Dynamo Dan will sort them out!

There wasn't a crisis or emergency too big for Stanley's dad. And there were a LOT of emergencies, believe me. So many that they all started to make Dynamo Dan a little ... tired.

That's right – even superheroes get tired sometimes. I know it's hard to believe, but it's true.

And that's why Dynamo Dan had a day off, every week. He didn't want to, but Stanley's mum put her foot down.

"I don't care if a hurricane is about to hit Hawaii," she yelled. "The bags under your eyes are bigger than suitcases. Every Friday you'll have a rest, or I'll hide your Dynamo Dan costume. You can spend some time with Stan."

Stanley was delighted. Of course he was. He loved spending time with his dad.

"After school, we can go to the park," Stanley told his dad with a grin. "Imagine how high you can push me on the swings with your super-strength ..."

"High enough to grab the moon!" Dad answered, with a yawn.

"Plus, there's the roundabout. One shove from you and it'll be like riding a rollercoaster."

"Deal," said Dad. "Then I'll take you for ice cream. How about that?"

"Brilliant!"

Stanley smiled. He was proud of having a superhero for a dad. Who wouldn't be? But sometimes it could be lonely too. Dad worked long hours and Stan wasn't allowed to ring him for a chat. It wasn't possible to answer a call while you were saving the world. Besides, Dad's costume had no pockets to put a phone in.

CHAPTER 2
FRIDAY ARRIVES!

Stanley could hardly wait for Dad's day off. On Friday he raced out of class to find Dynamo Dan in his everyday clothes, dozing against the school gates. Other parents stared and tutted at him, but it didn't bother Stanley. He leaped into his dad's arms with such force that he almost knocked him off his feet.

"Woohooo!" Stanley yelled. "Park!
Roundabout! Ice cream!!"

Dad yawned, then nodded, trying to
look more excited than sleepy.

Minutes later, the two of them were walking down the street. Stanley was talking faster than Dynamo Dan could fly as he filled Dad in on everything that had happened that week at school.

"I scored the winner at football today," he said. "A free kick, from outside the box. Then I drew a brilliant picture in class, then I got 10 out of 10 in a spelling test. Miss Almond thought I wouldn't be able to spell 'superhero', but – HA! She was wrong!"

Dad smiled and hugged Stanley. "What a week," he said. "Sounds much better than mine. I'd like to draw a picture sometimes, instead of stopping a runaway train, or holding up a bridge before it collapses."

Dad yawned again. Even the THOUGHT of what he'd done that week was tiring.

"Don't worry, Dad," Stanley said. "Soon we'll be at the park, and you can sit on the bench for a while. You don't have to push me on the swing. Not all the time anyway."

Stanley wasn't just being kind. He meant it. If Dad needed a rest that was fine by him. At least they were together.

CHAPTER 3
A MOGGIE GOES MISSING

Just as Dad and Stanley turned onto the high street, hand in hand, disaster struck. An old lady stood wailing on the pavement. She looked at least 117 years old. A crowd surrounded her, trying to calm her down.

"My cat!" she wailed. "My poor little kitty cat. He's stuck up a tree and I can't get him down."

"Oh no," a man in the crowd said. "What should we do? Climb up and fetch it?"

"He's right at the top," the old lady sobbed.

"We could shake the tree and hold out a huge blanket to catch him at the bottom," the man suggested.

"Never!" the old lady shrieked. She looked set to whack the man with her handbag for even thinking such a thing. "My cat is far too precious for such a risky plan."

"Well, we've only one option then, haven't we?" the man said. "We'll have to call for Dynamo Dan. He'll save the day."

'Oh no!' Stan thought. The last thing he wanted was for Dad to be needed on his day off. Mum would be cross and Dad would be too tired to take Stanley to the park.

So, instead, Stanley stole a glance
at Dad, who was now leaning on a
lamp-post half asleep. Then he pushed
his way into the crowd.

"It's no good calling for Dynamo
Dan," he told the crowd. "He's on his day
off – I mean, he's stopping a skyscraper
in Tokyo from falling down. But I can
help you. I'm a very good climber."

The crowd laughed, but Stanley wasn't put off. He'd rather climb a stupid tree and rescue a stupid cat than let them ruin his time with Dad.

"Where is the cat?" Stanley asked, and his chest puffed out like a brave superhero.

"Just round the corner," the old lady said.

And so Stanley marched on, and found not a cat, but a ... PANTHER. There, stuck up the tree, was a black panther!

Now, this would've been enough to send most children running home squealing for their mum, but not Stanley. He knew what he had to do.

CHAPTER 4
POUNCING ON A PANTHER

Stanley turned to the old woman.

"Don't worry, missus," he said in a calm voice. "I'll bring him down." Then he spotted some knitting needles sticking out from her bag. "May I borrow a ball of wool?" he asked.

The old woman could hardly say no. She handed the wool over, and watched as Stanley shimmied his way up the tree like a monkey.

On he climbed, not bothered by the height of the tree or the wind that blew at his hair. The sooner he brought the panther down, the sooner he and Dad would get to the park, and the sooner they could have an ice cream.

But the panther was not pleased
to see Stanley, and he growled like
Stanley's dad before he'd drunk his
morning cup of coffee.

"Well, there's no need for that!"
Stanley said as he sat on the branch

beside the panther. "'Hello' would've been a far kinder way to greet me. I've even brought you something to play with."

From his back pocket, Stanley pulled out the wool and waved it in front of the panther's nose.

Now, as everyone knows, cats LOVE to play with wool, no matter how big they are.

When the panther caught sight of the ball of wool in Stanley's hand, he turned out to be no exception. Gone was his bad mood, gone was the growling and the showing of teeth. Stanley was now his best friend in all the world.

What followed was a fun-filled but wobbly five minutes of play, as the pair batted the ball between each other. Only when the ball of wool fell off the branch and flew to the ground did the fun stop.

"Oh dear," Stanley sighed. "Looks like we'll have to finish the game down there."

But all of a sudden our panther friend seemed a bit scared, as if it had only just dawned on him that he was

20 metres off the ground. He put his front paws over his eyes and began to shake like jelly.

"It's OK," Stanley said. "There's nothing to be scared of. I'll give you a piggy back if you like."

What followed was the bravest thing the crowd had ever seen. Down the tree trunk slid not only a little boy, but a little boy with a shaking, shuddering panther on his back.

As Stanley's feet hit the ground, the old lady hugged him and the panther licked him.

"How can we ever repay you?" the old lady asked.

"All in a day's work, ma'am," Stanley answered. Then he walked modestly back through the crowd, to where his dad was snoozing gently.

"What happened? What did I miss?"
Dad grunted after Stanley had shaken
him awake.

"Oh nothing," Stanley told him. "Can
we go to the park now?"

CHAPTER 5
BATH TIME

On the pair walked, talking about their favourite ice cream flavours.

They hadn't gone far when Dad started to slow down. Stanley had no idea how he was doing it, but Dad seemed to be sleep-walking and talking at the same time.

"Chocolate …" Dad dribbled.

"Straaawberriezzzzzzzz."

48

Stanley sighed. The sooner he got some sugary ice cream into his dad the better! But as they crossed the road, a howl shattered the peace.

"Help! Help!" a man shouted. "A pipe has burst in our house and there's water dripping from the ceiling."

There was a crowd gathered round the man, shouting helpful advice like –

"Turn off the taps!"

And

"Have a shower in it!"

And

"Ring the fire brigade!"

Thankfully, one woman had some sense and told the man to call a plumber, but the man replied –

"She can't come till Monday. By then it'll be too late. That does it. There's nothing for it but to call for Dynamo Dan!"

This was enough to make Stanley rocket into action.

"No! You can't do that," he shouted. "He's too tire– I mean, he's too tied up, saving the world. I'll help instead."

And, with great bravery, Stanley
walked to the man's front door. He
peered in the letterbox, only to be
squirted in the face by the biggest jet of
water ever.

Stanley gasped. He couldn't believe
the mess inside. There was water
everywhere! Never mind a leaky pipe, it
looked like an ocean inside the house.

Stanley had to think on his feet. He did three things.

1. He shoved five sticks of bubble gum into his mouth and chewed as fast as he could.

2. He grabbed the lid off the dustbin in the front yard.

3. He climbed up the drainpipe and in the bathroom window.

"Geronimo!" he yelled, and he threw the bin lid onto the ocean of water and jumped on top of it as if it were a surfboard.

Stanley sped across the waves, swerving left and right, gazing in wonder as he spotted a jellyfish, a seahorse and even a shark swimming around!

But Stanley didn't have time to panic. He had to save the day and get him and his dad to the park before the ice cream van went home. Stanley kept his super-vision eyesight switched on, and at last he spotted the cause of the problem. There was a broken pipe at the top of the stairs.

Stanley zoomed forward on his surfboard, and dived into the water when he reached the pipe. Then he clambered up the banister and reached into his mouth to pull out the sticky gum. With speed and skill, Stanley stuck the gummy goo onto the pipe and pressed hard.

Within seconds, the pipe stopped gushing and the water, jellyfish, seahorses and even the shark all washed down the plughole.

The crowd outside went bonkers. And they screamed louder than ever when Stanley appeared outside.

"What a hero!" they yelled.

"What a star!"

"What a champ!"

Someone in the crowd even asked
if he was free to unblock their loo, but
Stanley shook his head and dashed off.
There was somewhere else he needed
to be.

CHAPTER 6
MONSTER TRUCK

Stanley found his dad snoring against a road sign. He woke him up and then blushed when Dad saw how wet he was.

"Car splashed me," he lied, and he began to pull Dad back in the direction of the park.

The finish line was in sight.

Stanley could see the top of the slide poking through the trees like a giraffe's neck. It wouldn't be long until Dad was spinning him madly on the roundabout.

But just as the pair approached the park gates, disaster struck. There was a huge BANG from around the corner. It was so loud that it pulled Dad from his daydream and scared Stanley half to death.

"What was that?" Dad asked, his superdad senses on high alert.

"Oh, it's probably nothing," Stanley fibbed. If there was a problem there was no way he was going to let Dad sort it out, not when the park was so close. "Tell you what, Dad, you rest

here a minute and I'll find out what's happened."

Before Dad could protest, Stanley sprinted off in the direction of the BANG. After 50 metres, he spotted a tough-looking man sitting on the kerb, with his head in his hands.

"My truck," he wailed. "My truck has a flat tyre and I'm meant to be racing it tonight. If I don't get there in time I won't get paid, and if I don't get paid then I can't feed my kids, and if I don't feed my kids then my wife won't love me any more."

Stanley felt for the man, he really did. He didn't want to see anyone so upset.

"I'll help you," he said, and he led the man round the corner to where his truck was parked.

But oh my goodness. This wasn't any old truck, oh no, this was a MONSTER TRUCK. Its four huge wheels were bigger than most people's houses!

But Stanley wasn't put off, not even for a second. Instead, he shrugged and walked towards the truck, spitting on his hands as he went.

Then, with the most incredible strength, Stanley lifted the back of the truck clean off the ground. "If I hold it up, maybe you can unbolt the wheel?" he asked the truck driver.

With wide goldfish eyes, the man tried to do as he was told.

What a sight it was to behold! A crowd gathered round the truck, gasping in delight at the amazing strength of the boy before them.

"Wow," they gasped.

"Golly."

"Gosh."

But the man who drove the truck wasn't quite as super as Stanley. No matter how hard he tried, he couldn't loosen the nuts enough to take off the wheel.

It was time for Stanley to come to the rescue ... again!

"Don't worry," he told the trucker. "Let me have a go. I bet you've loosened it already."

Brave and strong, Stanley took the weight of the truck with one hand, and with the other undid not only the first nut, but the second, third and fourth as well.

The crowd went CRAZY. They cheered and clapped and whooped, but all that did was make Stanley blush. He helped the trucker fit the new tyre, shook his hand and then weaved back through the crowd to find his dad, snoring like a buffalo with a bad cold.

"Come on," Stanley whispered, and he practically carried his dad into the park. "Before they start following us."

CHAPTER 7
THE DYNAMIC DUO

The park was looking glorious. The sun was out, shining bright onto the flowers and plants that burst from the earth.

'We've done it,' Stan thought with a smile. 'We got here without anyone bothering Dad. Now the fun can really start.'

With joy in his heart, Stanley bounded towards the swings. Even Dad was full of energy, running after Stanley to give him a push.

But no sooner had Stanley started swinging, than his ride came to a crushing halt.

As if from nowhere came a crowd of people. A HUGE crowd. The sort of crowd you find inside a football stadium. And they were all heading for Stanley's swing.

"There he is – look!" they yelled.

"Over there – I see him."

"I can't believe it. A superhero, a real-life superhero, and now we've found him."

"Oh no," Stanley said to himself. "This can't be happening."

He'd got Dad all the way to the park without a single superhero deed, and still the crowd recognised him! Stanley didn't know how this was happening. It wasn't like Dad was wearing his costume or his mask, so how had the crowd guessed that he was Dynamo Dan?

Stanley braced himself, ready to deny the crowd as they rushed towards his dad, holding out pens and camera phones, desperate for a magic moment with the great man himself.

But then something very weird happened.

The crowd reached Stanley's dad, but they didn't stop. Instead, they rushed past him towards Stanley, still cheering and clapping.

Stanley didn't know what to do. 'Is there another superhero behind me that the crowd's desperate to get to?' he wondered.

No. There was no one else behind him.

Word had spread of Stanley's acts of bravery, videos had been put on the internet – heck, he'd even made the News. And now everyone, absolutely everyone, wanted to shake his hand.

Stanley was spun round in a whirlwind of attention. There were requests for autographs and photos, people wanted interviews and kisses. Apart from the kisses, Stanley was sort of happy to oblige.

At least that was until a dark shadow fell across the park, a dark shadow that could only mean one thing. Earth was being invaded. Invaded by aliens. One glance up to the skies confirmed as much.

Stanley's heart pounded. He looked to Dad and nodded. Dad nodded back. Then, with no thought for their own safety, they ran towards the U.F.O.

Within seconds they were flying through the air, super-powers at the ready, the greatest crime-fighting double act ever.

Father and son.

Dan and Stanley.

Dynamo Dan and ... Super Stan!